The Theft of the Samurai Sword: JAPAN

Join Secret Agent Jack Stalwart

on his other adventures:

The Search for the Sunken Treasure: **AUSTRALIA**

The Secret of the Sacred Temple: **CAMBODIA**

The Escape of the Deadly Dinosaur: **USA**

The Puzzle of the Missing Panda: **CHINA**

The Mystery of the Mona Lisa: **FRANCE**

The Caper of the Crown Jewels: **GREAT BRITAIN**

Peril at the Grand Prix: **ITALY**

The Pursuit of the Ivory Poachers: **KENYA**

The Quest for Aztec Gold: **RUSSIA**

The Deadly Race to Space: **MEXICO**

The Fight for the Frozen Land: **ARCTIC**

The Theft of the Samurai Sword: JAPAN

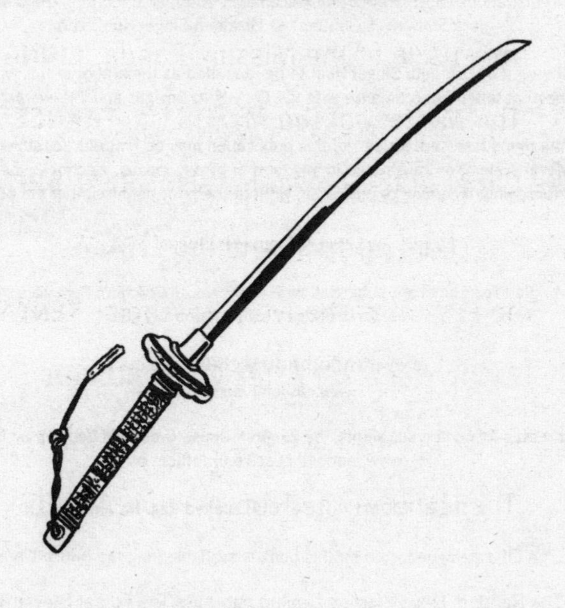

Elizabeth Singer Hunt

Illustrated by Brian Williamson

RED FOX

THE THEFT OF THE SAMURAI SWORD: JAPAN
A RED FOX BOOK 978 1 862 30635 6

First published in Great Britain by Red Fox,
an imprint of Random House Children's Publishers UK
A Random House Group Company

This edition published 2009

5 7 9 10 8 6

Set in 14/22pt MetaNormal

Red Fox Books are published by Random House Children's Publishers UK,
61–63 Uxbridge Road, London W5 5SA

www.**randomhousechildrens**.co.uk
www.randomhouse.co.uk

Addresses for companies within The Random House Group Limited can be found at:
www.randomhouse.co.uk/offices.htm

THE RANDOM HOUSE GROUP Limited Reg. No. 954009

A CIP catalogue record for this book is available from the British Library.

The Random House Group Limited supports The Forest Stewardship Council (FSC®), the leading international forest certification organisation. Our books carrying the FSC label are printed on FSC® certified paper. FSC is the only forest certification scheme endorsed by the leading environmental organisations, including Greenpeace. Our paper procurement policy can be found at
www.randomhouse.co.uk/environment

Printed and bound in Great Britain by Clays Ltd, St Ives PLC

For Max, Eve, Doug and Hilary

THE WORLD

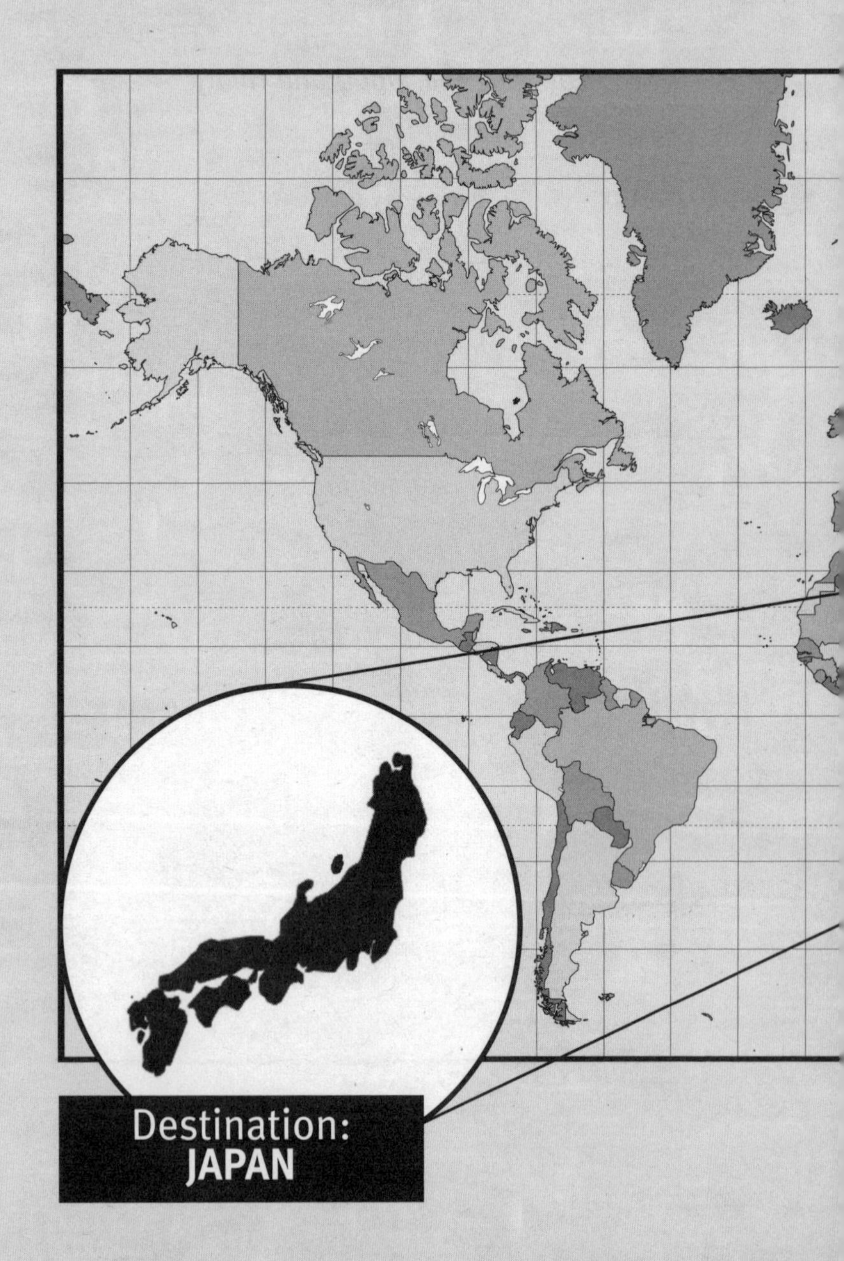

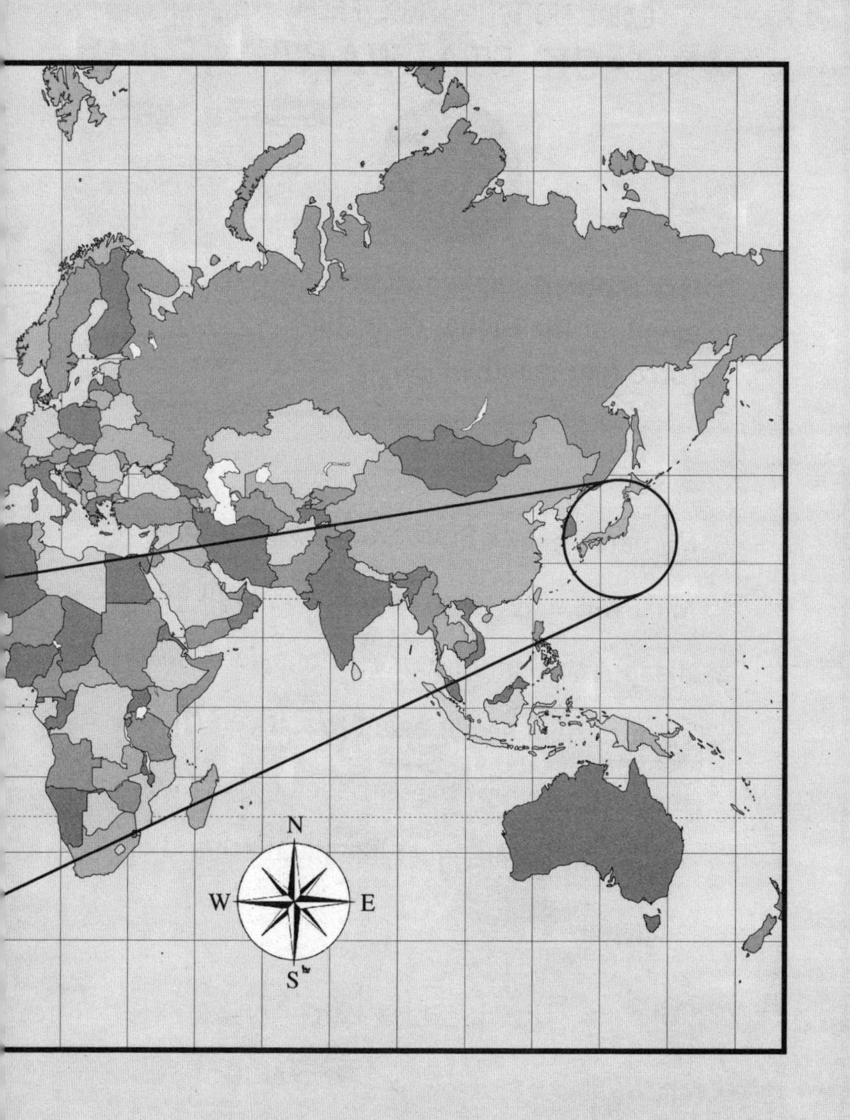

N
W
E
S

GLOBAL PROTECTION FORCE FILE ON

JACK STALWART

Jack Stalwart applied to be a secret agent for the Global Protection Force four months ago.

My name is Jack Stalwart. My older brother, Max, was a secret agent for you, until he disappeared on one of your missions. Now I want to be a secret agent too. If you choose me, I will be an excellent secret agent and get rid of evil villains, just like my brother did.

Sincerely,

Jack Stalwart

GLOBAL PROTECTION FORCE INTERNAL MEMO:

HIGHLY CONFIDENTIAL

Jack Stalwart was sworn in as a Global Protection Force secret agent four months ago. Since that time, he has completed all of his missions successfully and has stopped no less than twelve evil villains. Because of this he has been assigned the code name 'COURAGE'.

Jack has yet to uncover the whereabouts of his brother, Max, who is still working for this organization at a secret location. Do not give Secret Agent Jack Stalwart this information. He is never to know about his brother.

Gerald Barter

Gerald Barter
Director, Global Protection Force

THINGS YOU'LL FIND IN EVERY BOOK

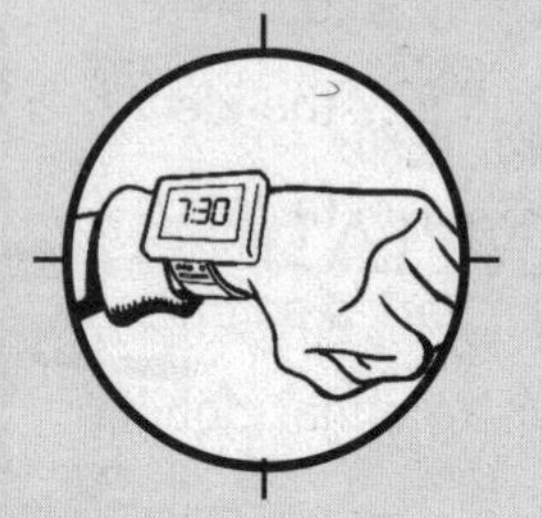

Watch Phone: The only gadget Jack wears all the time, even when he's not on official business. His Watch Phone is the central gadget that makes most others work. There are lots of important features, most importantly the 'C' button, which reveals the code of the day – necessary to unlock Jack's Secret Agent Book Bag. There are buttons on both sides, one of which ejects his life-saving Melting Ink Pen. Beyond these functions, it also works as a phone and, of course, gives Jack the time of day.

Global Protection Force (GPF): The GPF is the organization Jack works for. It's a worldwide force of young secret agents whose aim is to protect the world's people, places and possessions. No one knows exactly where its main offices are located (all correspondence and gadgets for repair are sent to a special PO Box, and training is held at various locations around the world), but Jack thinks it's somewhere cold, like the Arctic Circle.

Whizzy: Jack's magical miniature globe. Almost every night at precisely 7:30 p.m., the GPF uses Whizzy to send Jack the identity of the country that he must travel to. Whizzy can't talk, but he can cough up messages. Jack's parents don't know Whizzy is anything more than a normal globe.

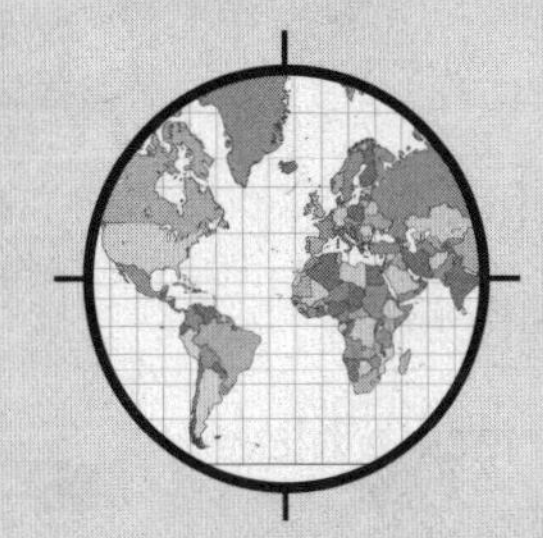

The Magic Map: The magical map hanging on Jack's bedroom wall. Unlike most maps, the GPF's map is made of a mysterious wood. Once Jack inserts the country piece from Whizzy, the map swallows Jack whole and sends him away on his missions. When he returns, he arrives precisely one minute after he left.

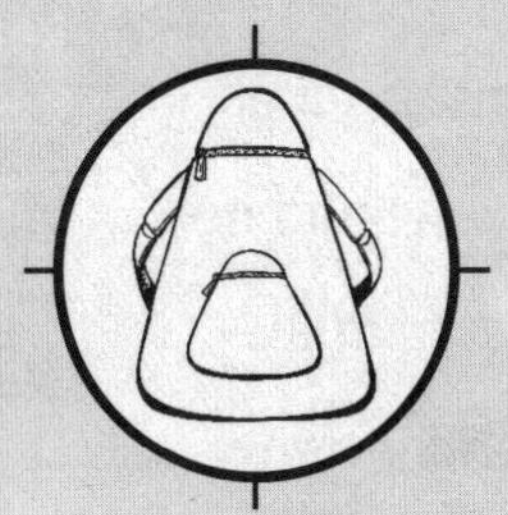

Secret Agent Book Bag: The Book Bag that Jack wears on every adventure. Licensed only to GPF secret agents, it contains top-secret gadgets necessary to foil bad guys and escape certain death. To activate the bag before each mission, Jack must punch in a secret code given to him by his Watch Phone. Once he's away, all he has to do is place his finger on the zip, which identifies him as the owner of the bag and immediately opens.

THE STALWART FAMILY

Jack's dad, John

He moved the family to England when Jack was two, in order to take a job with an aerospace company. Jack's dad thinks he is an ordinary boy and that his other son, Max, attends a school in Switzerland. Jack's dad is American and his mum is British, which makes Jack a bit of both.

Jack's mum, Corinne

One of the greatest mums as far as Jack is concerned. When she and her husband received a letter from a posh school in Switzerland inviting Max to attend, they were overjoyed. Since Max left six months ago, they have received numerous notes in Max's handwriting telling them he's OK. Little do they know it's all a lie and that it's the GPF sending those letters.

Jack's older brother, Max

Two years ago, at the age of nine, Max joined the GPF. Max used to tell Jack about his adventures and show him how to work his secret-agent gadgets. When the family received a letter inviting Max to attend a school in Europe, Jack figured it was to do with the GPF. Max told him he was right, but that he couldn't tell Jack anything about why he was going away.

Nine-year-old Jack Stalwart

Four months ago, Jack received an anonymous note saying: 'Your brother is in danger. Only you can save him.' As soon as he could, Jack applied to be a secret agent too. Since that time, he's battled some of the world's most dangerous villains, and hopes some day in his travels to find and rescue his brother, Max.

DESTINATION:
Japan

The Japanese flag is white with a red circle in the middle, symbolising the rising sun

•

The Japanese name for Japan is Nippon

•

Over 127 million people live in Japan

The tallest mountain in Japan is called Mount Fuji. It is over 3,700 metres tall

•

The capital city of Japan is Tokyo

•

Japan's currency is the yen

GPF Culture Guide: Japan
Eating and Karaoke

One of the most popular foods in Japan – and round the world – is sushi

Most people think of sushi as being fish and rice wrapped in pressed sheets of seaweed. But it can also be a bowl of rice topped with fish, meat or vegetables

Japanese people use chopsticks to eat their food

Karaoke – singing into a microphone whilst reading lyrics to a song on a video screen – started in Japan

GPF FAST FACTS: THE SAMURAI

The word 'samurai' means
'those who serve'

They were the warriors of Japan until
the late 1800s

In later years they won so many battles
and gained so much power that
they ruled Japan

The word 'bushido' means 'way of the
warrior' and refers to the code of
conduct the samurai lived by

The samurai used many weapons including
swords, bows, daggers and spears.
The most famous of all is
called a 'katana'

If you were born into a samurai family,
you received a sword when you turned
thirteen years old

SECRET AGENT PHRASEBOOK FOR JAPAN

SECRET AGENT GADGET INSTRUCTION MANUAL

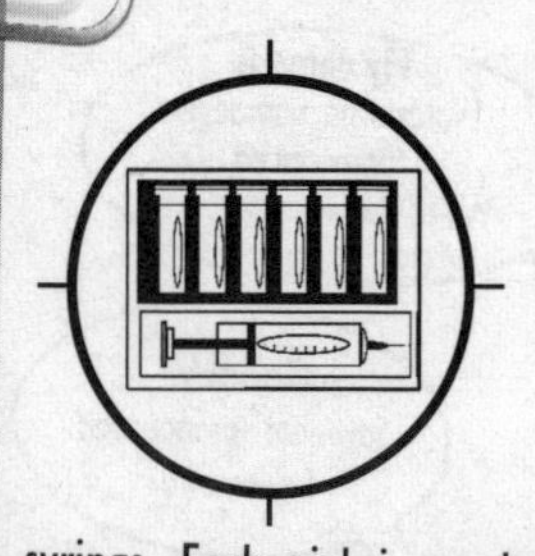

Antidote Pack: If you suspect that you've been poisoned, use the GPF's Antidote Pack to save your life. Figure out which part of your body is being affected and place the right vial in the syringe. Each vial is marked with a name of a body system: Cardiovascular, Immune, Muscular, Nervous, Respiratory, Skeletal. Jab the needle into the upper part of your bottom, and release the serum. It could take as long as 15 minutes to work.

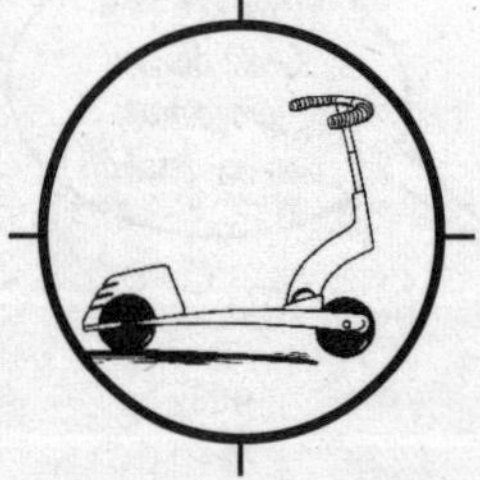

Scatta-Scooter: When you need to travel faster than your feet will take you, use the GPF's Scatta-Scooter. It looks like an ordinary scooter, but has a battery-powered engine fixed to the back. To re-charge, simply plug it into the mains for 1 hour.

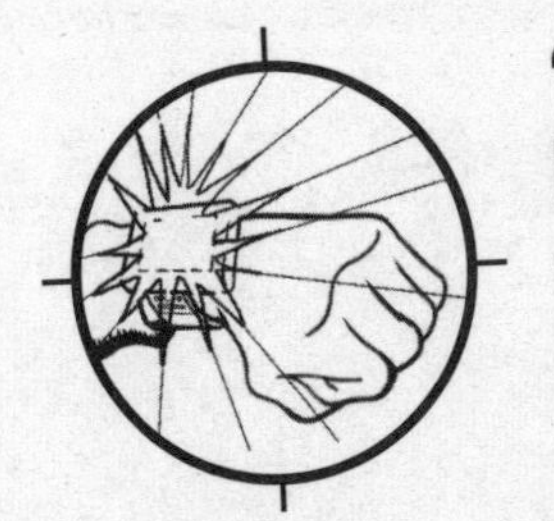

'Flash' on Watch Phone: Effective today, all Watch Phones will be updated to include a 'flash' feature. With it, an agent can send a high powered flash of light in short bursts. Perfect if you need to temporarily blind someone, or to send a rescue signal if you're lost at sea.

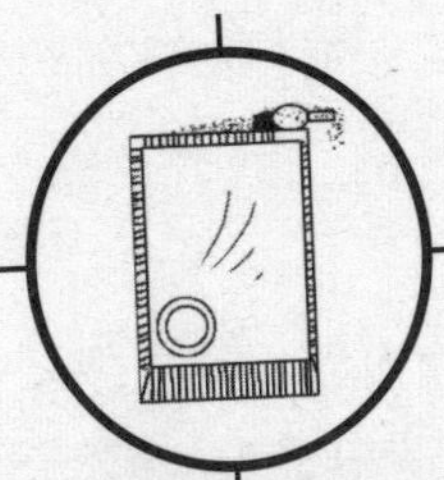

Wax Statue Dust: The GPF's Wax Statue Dust can freeze someone stiff for a period of 1 hour. Just sprinkle it over a person's head and within moments that person's skin and muscles will be completely still. Their insides however will remain fully functional.

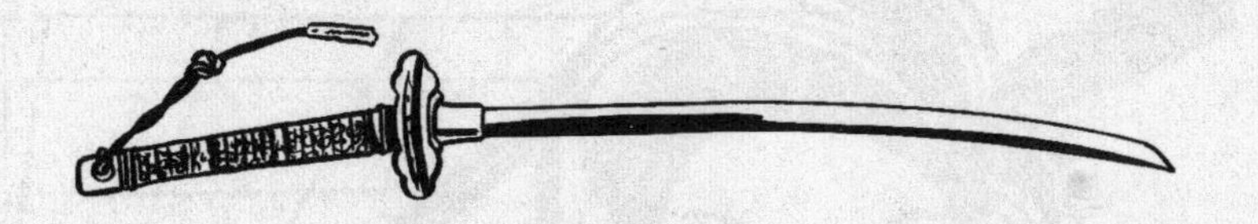

Chapter 1:
The Madame

It was a hot summer night in a far away country. A large lady wearing lots of make-up and a pretty kimono was sitting on top of a chair in the middle of a room. Her ruby-red lips parted, and she spoke to the four men standing before her. The men were dressed in black from head to toe. Hanging from their cheeks were black veils. The only thing you could see was their piercing dark eyes.

'OK, men,' she said. 'You've heard your instructions. Now go and claim my treasures.'

The men bowed and shouted the word 'hai' together. They held onto their batons, which were fixed to their sides, and then turned and ran out of the room.

Throwing her head back, the woman cackled with evil laughter. The glittery green powder that covered her eyelids sparkled in the light. As she brought her head forward, she smiled with smug satisfaction.

Now all Madame Midori had to do was sit back and relax. Within hours, her band of ninja thieves would return, bringing with them the treasures she so desperately wanted.

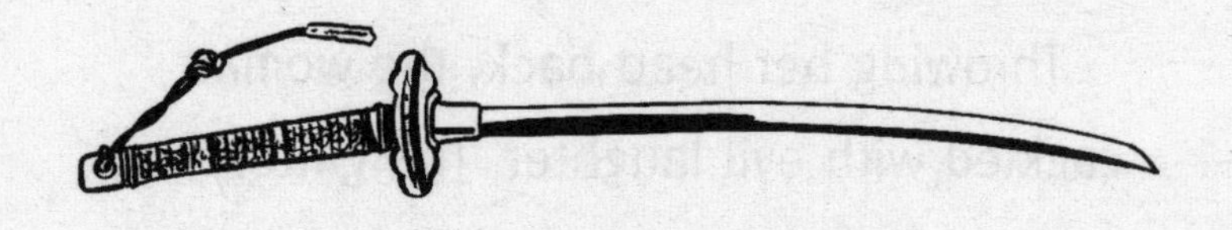

Chapter 2: The First Ninja

Within moments of leaving Madame Midori, ninja number one was hot on the job. He ran through the streets like a shadow, hopping over bins, surfing around cars and sneaking through parks and gardens.

Up ahead, he spied a two storey house with a red tiled roof. The house was surrounded by a high stone wall. This was the home of Mr. Taka, ninja number one's target.

Mr. Taka was a very wealthy businessman. He'd amassed so much money that he'd started to buy priceless works of art. Mr. Taka's private art collection was known throughout the world as one of the best. Because of this, some of his valuables were kept in a locked safe in his house.

Luckily for ninja number one, Madame Midori had done some work ahead of time. She'd obtained the layout of Mr. Taka's home (purchased for a large sum from the previous owner). She'd also given him an electronic code breaker (bought from an unsavoury character in the warehouse district).

Now all he had to do was get inside, and use his speed and skill to steal one particular object for Madame Midori.

He scaled the stone wall and jumped down to the garden below. Crouching low, he ran towards the house. Stopping underneath an open window on the second floor, he looked to the grounds to make sure no security was patrolling.

From the map Madame Midori had given him, ninja number one knew that the open window led to Mr. Taka's bedroom.

Satisfied that he was alone, ninja

number one shot a long nylon rope outwards from his hip. Attached to it was a metal claw. He waited for it to stick its teeth into the wooden window frame, and yanked on it to make sure it was stuck.

As he crawled over the window ledge and into Mr. Taka's house, he grinned. Success would soon be his.

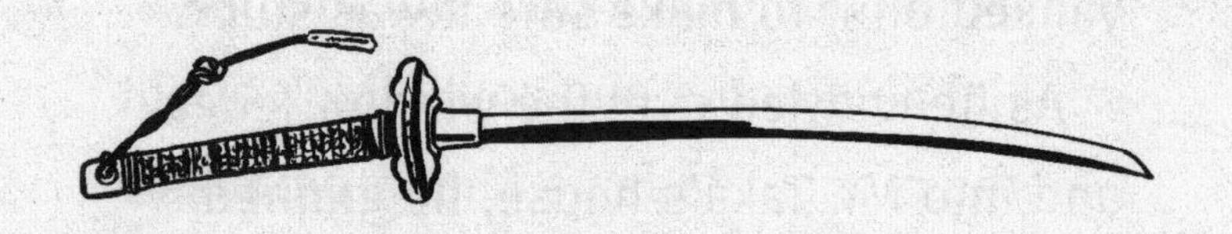

Chapter 3:
The First Theft

Ninja number one was part of a four man team hired by Madame Midori. They were asked to pull off one of the trickiest thefts in Japan's history – stealing four national treasures at the same time. While ninja number one was focused on Mr. Taka's house, the other men were scattered across Tokyo stealing priceless objects too.

Madame Midori called these men her

‘ninjas’ because they were trained in martial arts and practiced the ‘art of stealth’. For most people, being involved in something like this would lead to a feeling of shame and guilt. But the only thing ninja number one could think about was the money Madame Midori promised to put into his bank account when the task was done.

As he stepped onto Mr. Taka’s floor; he immediately looked to the bed. Mr. Taka was snoring like a bulldozer while Mrs. Taka slept peacefully by his side. Ninja number one shook his head in amazement. How someone could sleep so well next to something that noisy was beyond belief.

Thanks to a small nightlight plugged into the wall, ninja number one could see everything in the bedroom. Creeping like a cat, the thief walked over to a framed painting of a smirking woman dressed in brown.

Although it looked similar, he knew the real Mona Lisa hung in a museum in Paris. Madame Midori had bribed an old housekeeper to tell her where Mr. Taka's locked safe was. It was cleverly hidden behind this fake painting on the wall.

Sure enough, as he slid the framed painting to the left, it revealed an electronic safe. He hooked his code breaker over the key pad and within moments it had retrieved Mr. Taka's secret code. The safe was soon deactivated and the door to it popped open with a click.

At the noise, ninja number one glanced in Mr. Taka's direction. The man snorted and shuffled, and then went back to dozing noisily again.

The thief opened the safe and looked

inside. There, lying on its side and deep into the wall, was what he was searching for. He removed it from its hiding place, and took a good look.

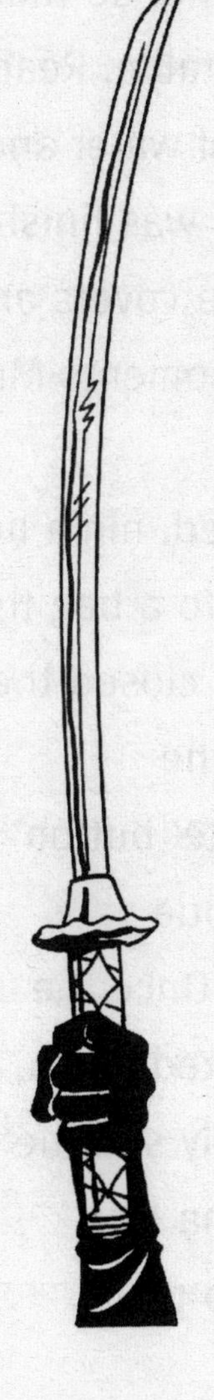

Its long wooden sheath was painted black. Decorating its gold handle were stones and expensive leathers. The curved steel blade inside glistened in the light when he pulled it out of its sheath. Although he felt no guilt in taking it, ninja number one felt awe in holding an ancient samurai sword that was over 600 years old.

Just then, Mr. Taka sat up in his bed. Ninja number one froze, nearly dropping the sword in fright. Mr. Taka twisted his body round, so that he was facing his bedside table. Reaching out, he grabbed a glass of water and drank it down. When he was finished, he crawled back under the covers and closed his eyes. Within moments Mr. Taka was snoring again.

Relieved, ninja number one stashed the sword into a bag that was strapped to his back. He closed the safe door and pushed the 'reactivate' button on his code breaker. Once the door locked again, he silently slid the fake Mona Lisa back into place.

All he had to do now was get out of there without being seen. He dashed to the window and stepped onto the ledge. Grabbing the rope, he swung down from the window and landed on the ground. As he yanked the metal claw from the window ledge, it made a sharp pinging noise.

The main light in Mr. Taka's bedroom window flickered on. Ninja number one could hear voices inside. The noise of that claw had woken them up.

Standing still, he was horrified to see Mrs. Taka peer from the window. She was looking outside for the source of the sound. Ninja number one tried to hide, but another light flickered on from a downstairs room. The only thing he could do was try to escape. He sprinted across the grounds and towards the stone wall.

Throwing his hands up, he climbed as

fast as he could up and over the stones. As he got to the ledge, he took a quick look in the direction of the house. Mrs. Taka was running around frantically, screaming. She'd seen the veiled intruder moving speedily across their grounds.

Ninja Number one jumped to the other side of the wall, but not before a piece of paper fell from his pocket. Unfortunately for him, he didn't realize it until he was nearly back at Madame Midori's. By then, it was too late to turn back.

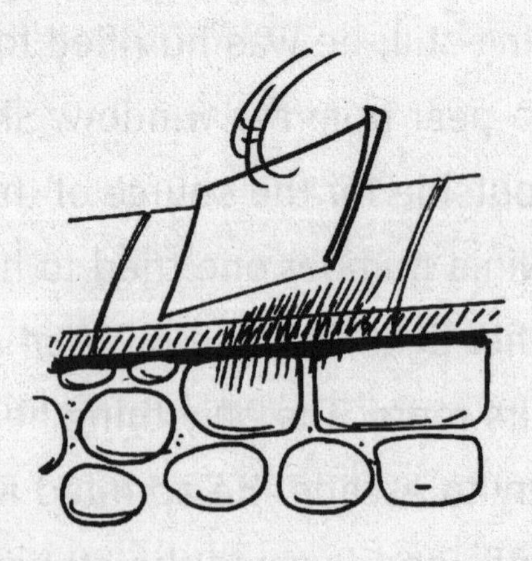

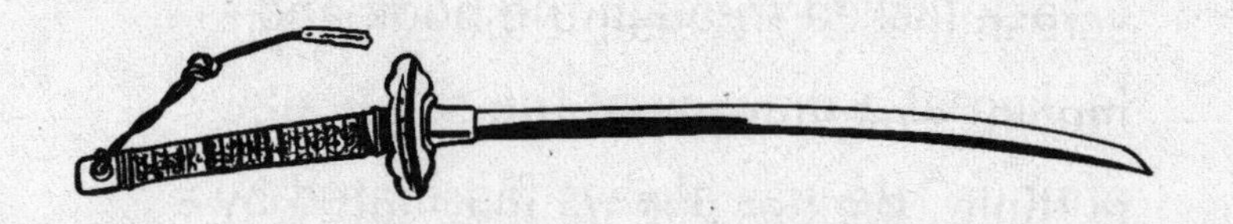

Chapter 4: The Warrior

At around the same time, but thousands of miles away, Jack Stalwart was sitting at his bedroom desk reading a book he'd checked out at the local library. It was called *The Samurai*.

The samurai were legendary fighters in Japan. They used to work for the lords and emperor, until they gained so much power that they ended up ruling the country themselves. The samurai (led by a shogun) ruled Japan for nearly six hundred years. In 1868 the last shogun gave up his power and Japan was ruled by an emperor again.

Jack flicked through the book and looked at a drawing of the samurai's armour. He was always fascinated by a warrior's dress. Samurai wore a helmet, shoulder and breast plates and guards for their arms, shins and thighs.

Although samurai used bow and arrows and spears, the *katana* was the most famous of all samurai weapons. It was a long, sharp sword. The picture in Jack's book was of a 15th century katana that belonged to a great samurai ruler.

At about the same time that Jack finished his book, he heard a sound coming from his bedside table. It was Whizzy, his magical miniature globe. Whizzy was starting to spin.

Besides Jack's Watch Phone and the secure website link, Whizzy was Jack's only connection with the GPF. It was through Whizzy that the GPF gave Jack the location of his next mission.

Jack was a secret agent for the Global Protection Force. The GPF was a worldwide force of secret agents responsible for protecting the world's most precious treasures. 'Protect that which cannot protect itself' was the motto of the GPF, and the code of honour that Jack and the other agents lived by.

He joined the force several months ago, when his brother Max (also an agent with the GPF) disappeared on one of their missions. Since then, he'd been gathering clues about his brother's whereabouts.

Until there was a break in that case, Jack had to fulfil his other secret agent duties. To that end, he turned his attention back to Whizzy who was spinning furiously.

Jack rushed over to his tiny globe. As he watched Whizzy twirl, he waited for him to do his thing. Whizzy coughed –

Ahem! A collection of small jigsaw pieces blew out of his mouth and onto the floor.

When he saw how many bits there were, Jack figured he was going to an island chain. He picked up the pieces, and carried them over to his Magic Map.

As he looked at the map that covered his wall, Jack tried to figure out where his mission could be. There was Indonesia, but that had more islands than Jack had in his hand. There was New Zealand but the shape of the country didn't fit. Finally, he looked at Japan. One by one, Jack placed the pieces in the right places.

Soon, the name Japan flashed from within that country and then disappeared again. Rushing over to his bed, Jack pulled his Book Bag out from underneath. He asked his Watch Phone for the code of the day. When he received the word SUSHI, he tapped it into his Book Bag's lock.

Instantly, the bag popped open. He checked to make sure everything was there. Jack noticed that several new gadgets - the Antidote Pack and Wax Statue Dust - had been added to his bag. He'd read about them in the latest GPF Gadget Instruction Manual. Excitedly, Jack locked his Book Bag again. Then he rushed back to the Magic Map.

The light inside Japan was glowing brightly now, illuminating his entire room.

When Jack was ready, he yelled 'Off to Japan!' and with that command, the light burst, swallowing him inside his Magic Map.

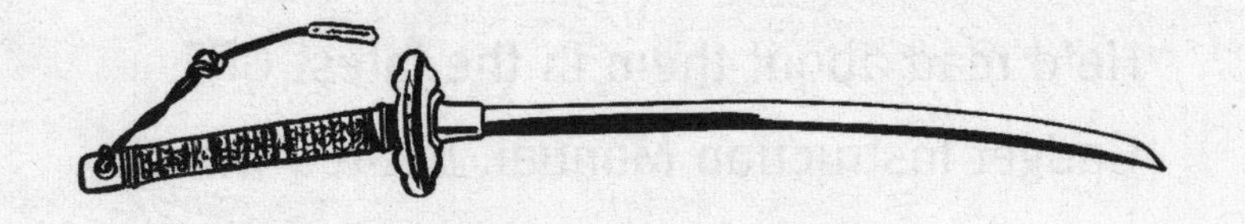

Chapter 5: The Commander

When Jack arrived, he found himself on a path next to a rectangular area filled with sand. Dotted throughout the sand were large rocks. Around the rocks, someone had raked the sand in circles.

As Jack looked at it, he realized that the sand looked like water, and the rocks looked like islands. Wondering whether this was arranged to look like the islands of Japan itself, Jack let his eyes scan his

surroundings. Elsewhere there were some maple trees and bamboo. There were also some stone Japanese lanterns dotted throughout.

Around the garden was a stone wall, and in front of him was a two storey house. There were red tiles on the roof and a red door at the front. He walked up to the door and knocked. He figured his contact was on the other side.

A man answered. He was tall and thin and dressed in a smart suit. Jack waited for him to say something first.

'Hello,' the man said in English. 'They're waiting for you upstairs.'

Jack was confused. Who were the 'they' and who was this man? Plus, how did he know to speak to Jack in English?

Jack stepped cautiously into the house. Spying some slippers on a step on the floor, Jack removed his boots and tucked them into his Book Bag.

Although it was customary to take off your shoes in a Japanese house, Jack didn't feel like leaving his life-saving GPF boots behind. After all, there were at least four gadgets tucked on the sides and in the soles of his boots.

'Follow me,' said the man once Jack had put on the slippers. Jack did as he was told. He followed the man – who he guessed must be a butler – down a long hallway and passed several rooms. The rooms had beige-coloured woven mats on the floor, and paper and wood doors that slid open.

They climbed some stairs at the end of the hall and entered a room full of Japanese policemen who also weren't wearing shoes. The butler left Jack, and returned to his duties downstairs.

Jack counted at least ten men. He gulped at the thought of why so many policemen were gathered in somebody's house.

'Ohayou,' said Jack, saying 'hello' in Japanese.

The men bowed and then moved apart, revealing another, more senior-looking man. Jack could tell he was more important, not only by the way the other men acted around him, but also by what he was wearing.

This man was taller than the rest, and had a crisp white shirt tucked underneath a dark jacket and trousers. He was also wearing a dark tie.

'Hello,' he said, as he bowed his head. 'We are so honoured that you could come to help us.'

Jack bowed back to the man, wanting to make sure he showed due respect.

'I am Superintendent General Ito,' the man continued. 'Chief of the Tokyo Police.'

Wow, Jack thought quietly to himself. Whatever happened here must have been serious. The boss of such a prestigious police force didn't show up unless the crime was really important.

'Tonight,' said the Chief, 'Japan has suffered a terrible series of crimes.'

'What's happened?' asked Jack.

The Chief shook his head. 'No less than four priceless Japanese treasures were stolen from museums and private collections across Tokyo.' He paused. 'All within half an hour of each other.'

'All at nearly the same time?' asked Jack. He couldn't believe one crook could pull off such an amazing feat.

'Yes,' Chief Ito said, 'unbelievable, right? We're thinking it was done by a team of thieves.'

'That would make sense,' said Jack.

'What did they take?'

'They took a beautiful antique kimono from the Museum of Tokyo,' the police chief replied. 'It was over 500 years old and was used in a Noh play.'

Jack knew that kimonos were a kind of robe worn by Japanese people. 'Noh' was a classic Japanese play acted out mostly by men.

'Also from the Tokyo Museum,' Chief Ito added, 'they stole a painting by Sesshū Tōyō, one of the most famous Japanese painters. From a Mrs. Sato they stole a priceless strand of cultured pearls.' Cultured pearls were perfectly round, and the process of making them was patented by a Japanese man in the early 1900s. 'And finally,' he added, 'they stole an ancient samurai sword from the man who lives in this house. Here's a picture of Mr. Taka's sword.'

The Chief showed Jack a colour photograph.

'I know this sword,' said Jack. 'It's from the fifteenth century, right?' Jack couldn't help but be shocked at the coincidence. This was the sword in his library book at home.

'Yes,' said the Chief. 'From what I understand, it was used by one of the most powerful samurai over 600 years ago. It is truly priceless.'

'Do you mind if I ask Mr. Taka some questions?' asked Jack. While he had no doubt the boss of the Tokyo police force had been thorough, he wanted to interview the owner of the sword himself.

Chief Ito nodded and motioned for Jack to enter another room.

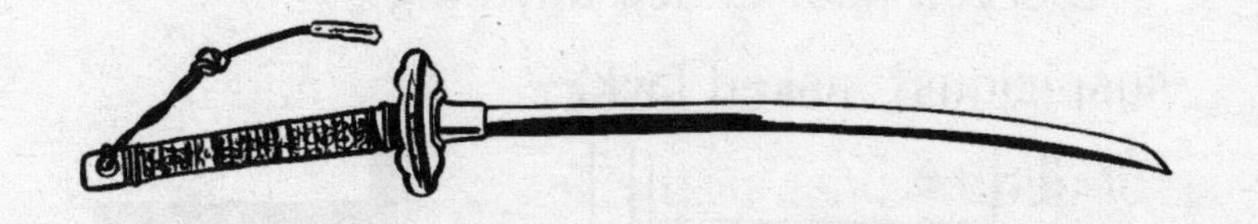

Chapter 6: The Sobbing Man

Jack went into Mr. Taka's bedroom and found the man sitting on the edge of his bed. He was still in his pyjamas, and was sobbing uncontrollably into his hands. His dutiful wife was trying to comfort him.

'Ohayou,' Jack gently said to the man.

Mr. Taka stopped crying for the moment and looked up at Jack. His face was red and wet with tears.

'I understand your sword was stolen in

the middle of the night,' said Jack.

The man nodded 'yes'.

'Was anything else taken?' asked Jack.

The man shook his head 'no'.

'Did you hear or see anything suspicious?' asked Jack.

Mr. Taka's wife piped up. 'I saw a dark shadow running across our garden and towards the wall,' she said. 'He jumped over it and ran away with our sword.'

Hearing this reminder, Mr. Taka started sobbing all over again.

Jack left them alone and walked up to Chief Ito.

'Have you checked the grounds?' Jack asked.

'Yes,' he replied. 'One of the first things we did after fingerprinting the room. There was nothing there, nor anything in the house. It's the same at each of the four crime scenes. The crooks left nothing behind.'

Jack didn't necessarily believe that. There was always some sort of clue to be found. With the focus of the detective work going on inside Mr. Taka's bedroom, Jack decided to take a look outside.

'Do you mind if I examine the grounds?' asked Jack.

'By all means,' said the the Chief. 'We're finished up there. If you find

anything come back and tell me, or give me a call.'

He handed Jack his business card with his contact details.

'I understand from the GPF that you're used to working on your own,' he said. 'I hope you can appreciate that I can't give you any of my men. The entire Tokyo police force is spread thin across the city, interviewing people and trying to solve these crimes.'

'No problem,' said Jack. 'I understand you have your hands full.'

Chief Ito turned away from Jack and took an urgent call on his cell phone. Jack made his way down the stairs, and changed out of the slippers and back into his boots. It was time to get to work.

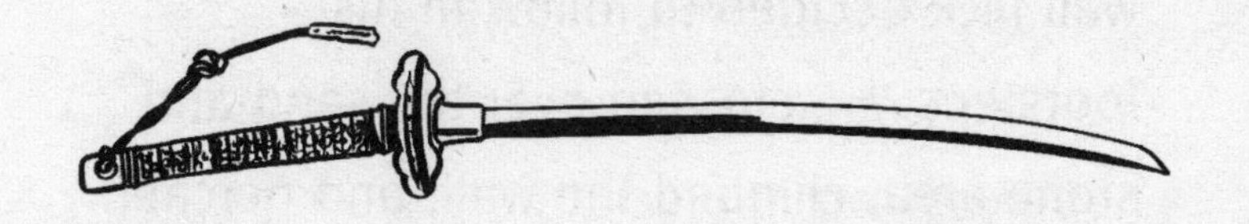

Chapter 7: The Lead

Jack left the house, walked into the garden, and stood under Mr. Taka's opened bedroom window. From below, Jack could see the teeth marks made by the claw that had lifted the crook into Mr. Taka's house.

There were a few messy footprints on the ground below the window, but nothing more to give Jack any clues. He traced the path from the window to the wall. When he got to the wall, he looked around. There were no obvious clues there either.

Since the thief escaped by climbing the wall Jack decided to follow in his footsteps. He crossed over the sand and stone area, climbed the wall, and perched himself at the top. From there, he could see Mr. Taka's bedroom window.

For a moment, Jack made himself think as if he was the thief. He wondered whether the burglar grew nervous when Mrs. Taka saw him at the wall. Jack looked to the ground on the other side. But there was nothing there. Maybe the Chief was right. Perhaps, Jack thought, the thief hadn't left any clues.

Just as Jack was about to climb down, he spied a white piece of paper resting on the top of the wall. He reached over to pick it up. Opening it, Jack tried to make sense of the Japanese characters scribbled on the note. But he wasn't able to read Japanese.

He pulled out his Secret Language Decoder and scanned the gadget from right to left over the writing. (In Japan everything was written from right to left).

Within moments, Jack's gadget had translated the scribble into a language that Jack could understand. The middle of the screen said:

THE GOLDEN DUCK

Jack couldn't be sure that this piece of paper had been left by the thief, but it was all he had to go on. He picked up his Watch Phone and called Chief Ito. When he picked up, Jack told him about the note. He asked whether the police chief knew what 'The Golden Duck' meant.

'Well,' he said, 'I'm not sure. There's a karaoke club called The Golden Duck in Tokyo. Maybe it refers to that place.'

'I'll check it out,' said Jack. 'This could lead us to more information about the team that committed these crimes.'

'You do that,' said Chief Ito. 'Let me know what you find out.'

'Will do,' said Jack, as he signed off.

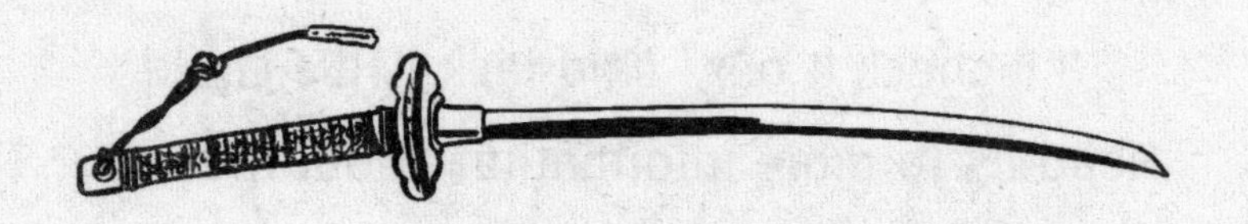

Chapter 8: The Route

The next thing Jack did was pull out his Map Mate. Every GPF agent was given one of these clever, handheld devices. It could tell you how to get from point 'A' to 'B' using arrows. It did this thanks to satellites in Space that fed information into the device.

He input the name 'The Golden Duck' and told it to search the city of Tokyo. Within seconds, his Map Mate had

calculated his route.

According to his gadget, it would take about an hour to get there by foot. Jack didn't need the power of his Flyboard, so he pulled out something that was less robust. It was called the Scatta-Scooter.

The GPF's Scatta-Scooter looked like an ordinary scooter, but it had a battery powered engine attached to the back.

It wasn't as fast as the Flyboard – it could only do up to fifteen miles per hour. But for a job like this, where he didn't want to draw too much attention to himself, it was perfect.

Snapping it together, Jack hopped on. He put on his Noggin Mould, hooked his Map Mate to the handlebars and took off.

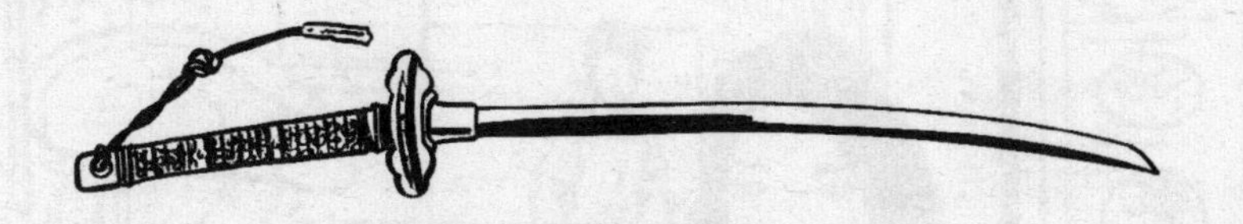

Chapter 9: The Club

Jack cruised from the residential areas around Tokyo and into the main city itself. This was the capital city of Japan. As far as Jack was concerned, it was one of the most exciting cities he'd ever seen.

There were neon lights all round and music playing from inside shops. People were bustling everywhere. There were stores selling funky clothes, music devices and even robotic dogs. He cruised

by a restaurant selling sushi rolls, or rice and avocado wrapped inside seaweed.

The red light on the Map Mate was blinking, which told Jack he was close. He slowed down his Scatta-Scooter, turned it off and packed it away.

He walked over to a glittering door with an awning over it. There was a sign on it, written in English for the tourists.

The Golden Duck

Tokyo's Most Famous Karaoke Club

Open 24 hours

Come inside

This was it. This was the name on the paper. Jack did what the sign said and entered the club. As soon as he did, he was overwhelmed by noise.

It was lunchtime, and The Golden Duck was really buzzing. There was a main stage in the middle of the room. A TV screen hung from the ceiling to the left. On the screen were words to songs written in both Japanese and English.

Jack knew exactly what this was about. His buddy Richard had introduced him to the idea of karaoke back home in England. When Richard turned eight, his Mum had bought him a karaoke machine. Since then, Jack, Charlie and Richard had spent hours singing old songs from when their parents were young.

All you had to do was sing to the words on the TV screen. If you did it right, you'd sound just like the people that created

the song in the first place. It was a fantastically funny thing to do. And it had been created right here in Japan.

An older man dressed in a suit made his way to the stage. He stood in front of the microphone, and the music started to play. It was the song 'Summer Nights' from the 1980s movie 'Grease'.

The man wiped the sweat off his brow and began to sing. Although he was trying his best, Jack couldn't help but think the man sounded like a strangled chicken.

Making his way across the room, Jack walked over to a man making drinks at the bar. He asked the man where he could find the owner of the club.

'There she is,' he said, pointing to a large woman. The older man had finished his song, and this woman was stepping onto the stage.

'That's Madame Midori,' he said. 'One

of the best karaoke entertainers in all of Tokyo.'

She grabbed the microphone as another song came on. It was 'I Will Survive' by a lady named Gloria Gaynor. Jack had heard his Mum sing it around their house.

Madame Midori began to belt out a tune. As she sang, Jack couldn't believe how good it sounded. The green eye shadow on her lids glistened in the light of the disco ball overhead.

When she finished, the crowd went wild. She lapped up their applause and then spoke into the microphone in English.

'Thank you all for coming,' she said. Then she waved to the audience and left the stage.

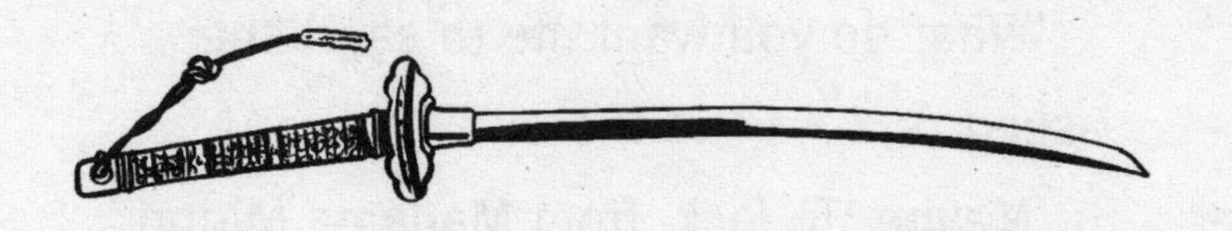

Chapter 10: The Fateful Meeting

Jack caught up with the woman as she was walking away.

'Madame Midori,' he said. 'I'd love to speak with you.'

The woman pulled a pen from her pocket and lifted it towards Jack.

'Where do you want me to sign?' she asked.

'Huh?' said Jack. He was a bit confused.

'You want my autograph, right?' she said.

'Oh, yes,' Jack said, not wanting to offend her. He scraped together a bit of paper from his trouser pocket and handed it to her.

'What do you want me to say?' she asked.

'Maybe 'To Jack, from Madame Midori,' he said.

'Very well then,' she said as she scribbled.

'Could I ask you a few questions?' asked Jack.

'Sure,' she said.

'A piece of paper with your club's name on it was found at the scene of a major theft last night,' said Jack.

At that, Madame Midori stopped signing her name.

'What do you mean?' she said, quickly and sharply.

'I've been asked by the Chief of the

Tokyo Police to follow up a lead,' offered Jack. 'It seems that a crook who stole an antique samurai sword last night had the name of your club on a piece of paper he carried with him.'

Madame Midori looked gravely at Jack.

'That's very odd news,' she said. 'I can't imagine why.'

'Well,' said Jack. 'Maybe he worked here. Can you think of anyone that you've hired recently that could be a suspect?'

'No,' she said, starting to shift away from Jack.

'Well,' Jack pressed on, 'is there anyone you can think of who's visited your club recently that may have committed a crime like this?'

'None that I can think of,' Madame Midori said. She paused for a moment, and then her eyes lightened again.

'You know,' she said. 'It's very noisy in here. I think it might be best if we talk in a quieter place. You're obviously visiting from out of town, why don't you meet me at my home? Then we can talk things through.'

Jack thought it was a good idea. It was definitely noisy here in the club.

'OK,' he said.

'Here's the address,' said Madame Midori. She handed Jack a card with an address written in English and Japanese.

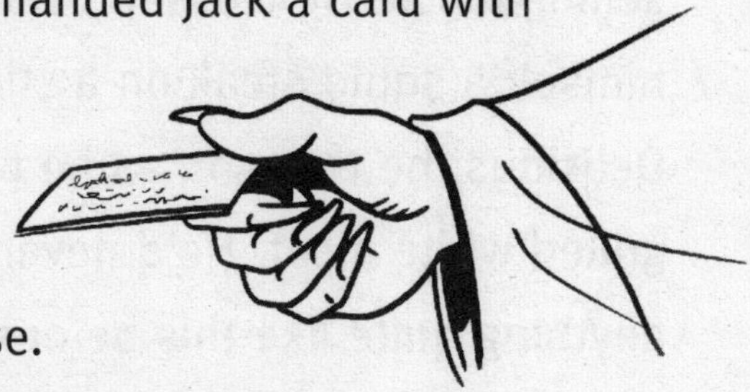

'Why don't we meet there in, say, fifteen minutes,' she said.

'Great,' said Jack. He figured the time would give him the chance to collect his thoughts and prepare a more thorough list of questions.

Jack said goodbye to Madame Midori, who soon vanished to somewhere else in the club.

He stepped outside and caught a breath of fresh air. Programming his Map Mate for Madame Midori's home, he saw that it would take only ten minutes to get there. That meant he had a few more minutes to kill.

Across the road, he spied a vendor selling lunch. He crossed over and bought himself a squid steak on a stick. Delicious, he thought, as he bit into the grilled white meat. He'd never tasted anything quite like this before.

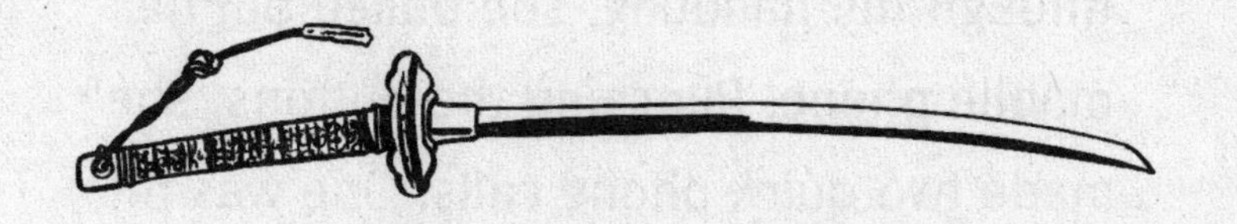

Chapter 11: The Decision

Madame Midori fumed as she left. How on earth did that pip squeak find out where she was? It must have been that idiot, ninja number one, dropping that piece of paper. This wasn't the first time he'd done something stupid. She'd deal with him and his clumsiness later.

For now, she had to focus on that kid. She needed to figure out a way to throw him off her trail, or better yet get rid of

him all together.

Soon, an idea popped into her mind. Madame Midori hurried to her car and climbed into the driver's seat. Fumbling through her handbag, she pulled out her mobile phone. Punching the buttons, she made two quick phone calls. One was to a local fishmonger; the other was to a member of her ninja gang. This kid and his snooping had to be stopped.

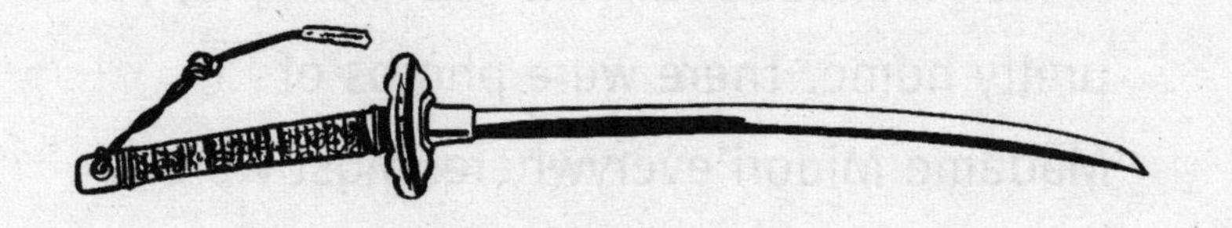

Chapter 12:
The Fugu

After finishing his snack, Jack hopped back onto the Scatta-Scooter and made his way over to Madame Midori's home. It was in a quieter part of town.

Jack walked up to the front door and knocked. Madame Midori opened the door and grinned.

'Hello!' she said. She seemed very excited to see Jack. 'Why don't you come in?'

Jack changed from his boots into the guest slippers, and followed Madame Midori through the building.

Jack looked around. It was a simple, yet pretty home. There were photos of Madame Midori everywhere. Most were of her singing into a microphone at her club.

'I am quite the karaoke entertainer,' she said proudly. 'I have won many singing competitions.'

Jack pretended that he was impressed. They moved through the house and towards a grand room at the back. There was an ornate table in the middle and a large decorated chair against the back of the wall. Leading from the room was a sliding door that led to an outdoor garden.

'Please,' Madame Midori said, 'why don't you sit down?'

Jack knelt down on the mat and faced the table.

'I have asked my chef to prepare a special delicacy for you,' she said, kneeling across from Jack. 'It's a special Japanese fish called Fugu.'

Jack had never heard of Fugu. He knew that in Japan a lot of interesting things were eaten, many of which he'd never tried before.

'Thank you,' he said. 'That's really nice of you to organize this for me. But I really just wanted to ask you some quick questions.'

'We can do that in a little while,' she said. 'Here's some tea.' She poured a cup of Japanese tea for Jack. He politely sipped a bit, although he didn't really like the taste of it.

'So anyway,' Jack started. He wanted to hurry up the questioning. Jack didn't want to spend all day in Madame Midori's home.

'I wanted to show you this piece of paper,' he said, opening the paper he'd taken from Mr. Taka's wall. 'Do you recognise the handwriting?'

'No,' she said, studying the paper. 'I'm sorry.' Not only was Madame Midori a good singer, she was also well-practised in the skill of acting.

A man entered the room. He was dressed all in black and was carrying a tray with a single plate on it.

'Aha!' she said. 'Here's the fugu. I'm a bit full right now, so I'll let you eat it all by yourself.'

Jack was pretty full too. After all, he'd just had a tasty squid snack. But he didn't want to insult his host. He smiled and said 'Itadaki-masu' which meant 'thanks for the food.'

Using chopsticks, he grabbed onto the fleshy meat. He bit into the Fugu and then started to chew.

Madame Midori looked at him. A smirk grew across her face. 'I hope you enjoy your food,' she said. Her smirk turned into a sinister growl. 'It will be the last thing you ever eat.'

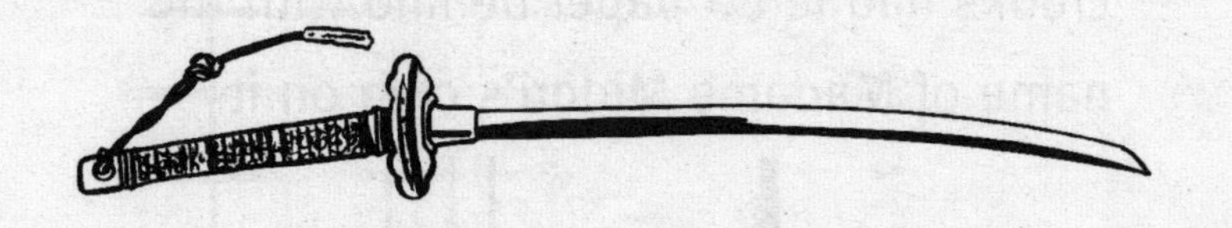

Chapter 13: The Poison

As soon as Jack heard this, he quickly spat out his food. What was she talking about? And why was she saying such nasty things? Madame Midori started to cackle with laughter.

Thoughts started rushing through Jack's head. He looked at the 'chef' that had brought him his food. He was dressed all in black. Mrs. Taka had seen a black shadow scurry across her garden. Another three figures came into the room and stood behind Madame Midori. Jack counted four men in total. There were four thefts in Tokyo last night. One of the crooks had left a paper behind with the name of Madame Midori's club on it.

Did Madame Midori hire these men to do her dirty work? Could Madame Midori be behind the most daring theft in Japanese history?

'There's no use fighting it,' she said. 'The poison of the puffer fish, or fugu, will kill you. It will paralyse your muscles and soon you will stop breathing.'

Jack had to react – and fast. He dashed from the room and threw his body through the paper door that led to the garden. Tumbling forwards, Jack landed near a pond filled with Koi, another kind of Japanese fish.

'Leave him be. We can clean up his body later.' Madame Midori snarled at the ninjas.

With Madame Midori and her goons inside, Jack was left alone in the garden. Already his lips and tongue were tingling. His throat was starting to go numb, sweat was coming out of his skin.

Reaching for his Book Bag, Jack pulled out his Antidote Pack and ripped open the box. He grabbed the syringe and looked for the antidote vial that he needed.

Jack could tell from his symptoms that the Fugu contained a poison that affected his nervous system. It was stopping all communication from his nerves to the other parts of his body.

He plunged the vial marked 'Nervous' into the syringe, and then pulled down his trousers a bit. He knew the fastest way to get the antidote into his body was to stick a needle in the upper part of his bum.

He pressed the tab on the top of syringe and released the serum into his veins. Jack's muscles started to shake and spasm. His heart rate began to drop. These weren't the side effects of the antidote. These were the fatal symptoms of the Fugu's poison. The antidote wasn't working quickly enough.

Jack could feel his body being paralysed. His muscles stiffened and he collapsed, finding it more and more difficult to breathe.

He tried to send kind thoughts to his mum, his brother, his father and his friends. In the background, he could hear Madame Midori. She was telling her men to 'hurry up and pack away the treasures.'

If Jack had a last wish, he wanted to

use it to get better. Most of all, he wanted to catch Madame Midori and make her pay for what she had done. Jack drew some shallow breaths and closed his eyes. It was time to let fate take its course.

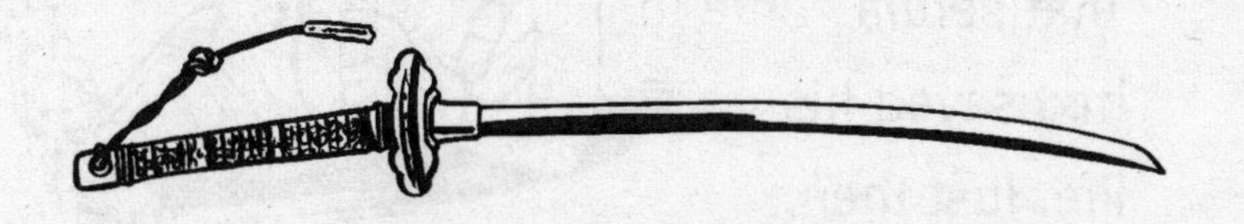

Chapter 14: The Recovery

As Jack lay there, he paid attention to the length of each of his breaths. After a little while, they seemed to grow longer and deeper. With each long breath, Jack's body felt a bit better.

The tingling in his tongue and lips eventually disappeared and his muscles started to grow stronger. In fact, he was able to sit himself upwards. All totalled, Jack figured that about ten minutes had

passed. Thank goodness for the antidote, he thought. That serum had saved his life. Just then, he could hear Madame Midori. She was still barking commands at her men. Jack had to stop them now, or else the priceless treasures may never be seen again.

Jack called Chief Ito, whose voice mail was on. Jack left him a message and told him what happened. He asked him to send reinforcements, and gave him the location of Madame Midori's house.

Jack crept through the garden and hid under one of the windows. Peeking inside the house, he could see the ninjas putting the samurai sword, painting, kimono and pearls in cardboard boxes.

If Jack had any doubts about who was responsible, seeing this proved that Madame Midori was the mastermind behind the thefts.

Just then, he heard the woman. 'Go outside and check for that boy,' she ordered. 'We need to get rid of him before anyone notices.'

Jack watched as two of the ninjas left the house, slid open the broken door and stepped into the garden. They looked to the area around the pond.

Since they knew that poison paralysed its victims, they were surprised to see no one on the ground. They went back into the house to report that fact to Madame Midori.

'He's not there,' said one.

'What do you mean, he's not there?' Madame Midori screeched in a huff. She left the house and looked for herself. When she couldn't find Jack anywhere, she became angry.

'Well find him!' she said. 'He can't have gone far!' Storming back into the house, she went about overseeing the remaining packing.

The two ninjas returned to the garden. They began to look over the pond area again. Seeing them gave Jack an idea. If he could quietly trap these two, he could sneak into the house and catch the others later.

He reached into his Book Bag and pulled out his Net Tosser. The GPF Net Tosser was one of those gadgets that came in useful on nearly every mission. It was a disc with an internal net that sprayed over crooks and caught them inside.

Jack crept towards the men slowly. Just as he was about to activate the Net Tosser, Jack accidentally stepped on a twig.

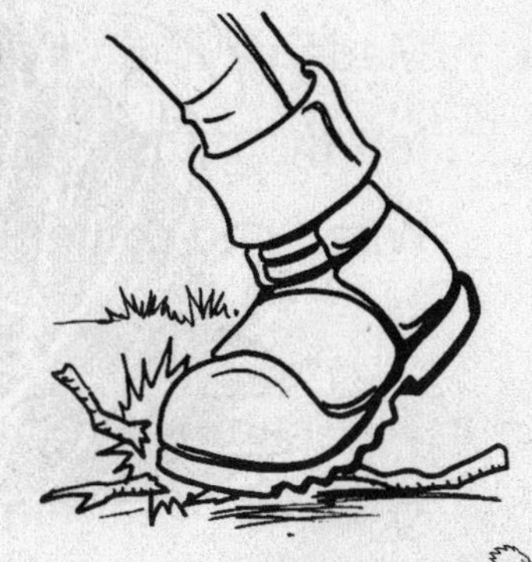

SNAP!

It was a quiet sound that made a big impact.

Instantly, the men turned towards Jack. For a moment they were shocked – after all, how did Jack survive? Their shock gave way to anger, and they ran towards Jack.

Quickly, Jack flung the Net Tosser their way. The long arms of the gadget reached out for the men, swirled around them, and then trapped them inside. The ninjas struggled helplessly, but they were definitely out of action.

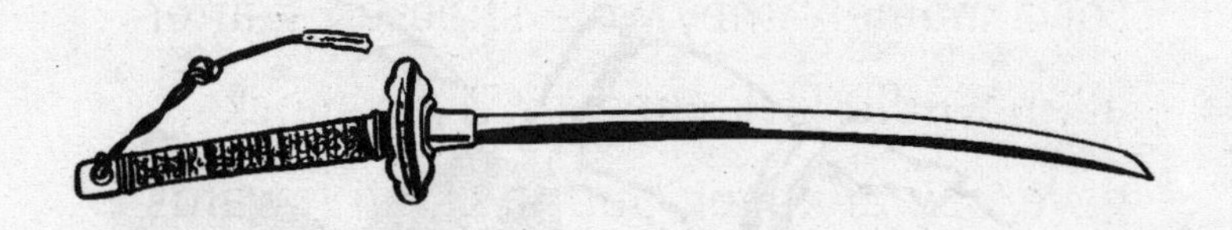

Chapter 15: The Second Round

The commotion outside had alerted the others that something was going on. This wasn't over yet, and Jack knew it. There were still two other ninjas and Madame Midori to deal with.

The first to come out were the ninjas. When they saw their buddies trapped in that net, they leapt over the pond and headed straight for Jack.

Jack ran in the other direction, but he

tripped on a stone. His body flew forwards and his stomach landed in the dirt. Scrambling, he tried to get up but one of the ninjas grabbed onto his foot.

'You're not going to get away from me!' he yelled. 'I've got too much money at stake!'

'Take that!' said Jack, as he kicked the man in the nose.

'Oww!' wailed the ninja.

With ninja number one tending to his bloody nose, Jack got to his feet again and started to run. Ninja number two was still chasing Jack.

Jack headed for a stone lantern just ahead. Looking over his shoulders, he could see the thug chasing from behind. Jack grabbed onto the top of the lantern and swung his body round, kicking the man in the gut as he passed.

'Arrgh!' yelled the ninja, as he tumbled backwards.

Jack let go of the lantern and landed on his feet. Now he was in the middle of the two men. One had a bloody nose and the other had a hurt tummy. Needless to say, they weren't happy. They raised their batons and scowled at Jack. The two crooks already under the Net Tosser were cheering their other ninja friends on.

In times like these, the GPF usually told their agents to do their best to use one of their gadgets. After all, two adult men against one boy were pretty tough odds. But Jack couldn't think of a gadget that would get them both, especially since they were at opposite ends of the path.

Jack was going to have to defend himself. Thankfully his judo instructor Mr. Baskin had taught him a thing or two. It was time to try out some new moves...

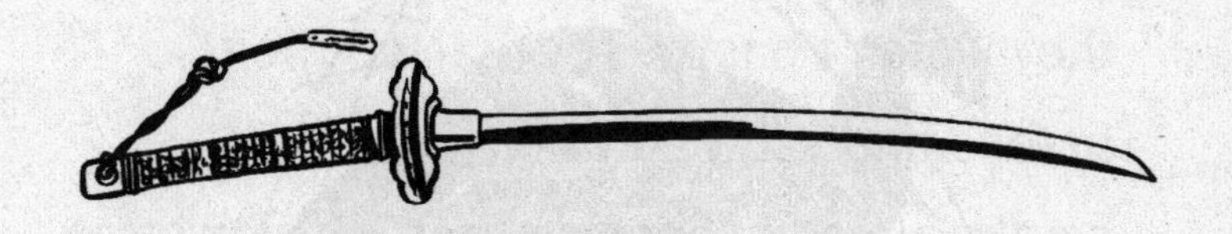

Chapter 16: The Moves

Ninja number one and his bloody nose made his move.

'I told you to get lost,' he growled. 'You're not going to get in the way of my money!'

He lifted his baton and lunged at Jack. As he ran for him, Jack grabbed onto the man's sleeves. He slid on his heels, and as he was about to land on his bottom, yanked the man over his shoulders.

The man came tumbling forwards and onto his back. This was called the 'side drop' in judo.

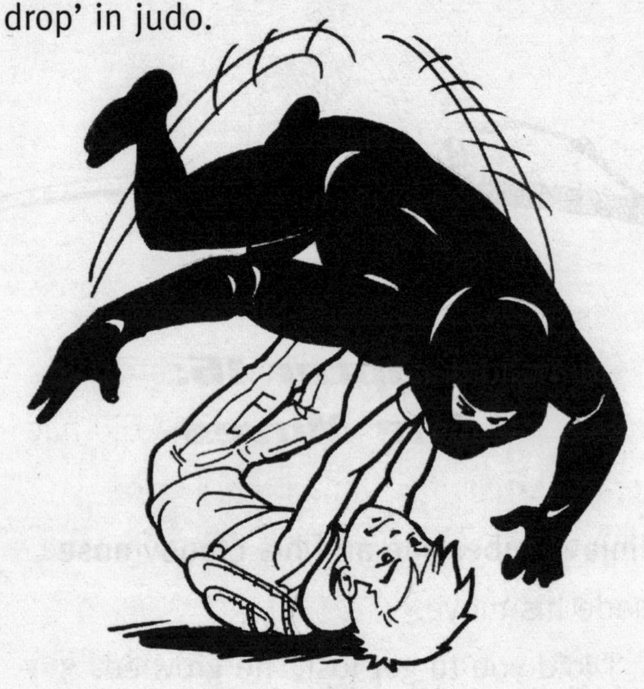

With his mate on the ground, the other ninja aimed for Jack, who quickly scrambled to his feet. But it wasn't fast enough. The man grabbed onto Jack's belt with his right hand, lifted him with his left, and then threw him onto the ground and onto his back.

‘Uggh,’ Jack said to himself. That really hurt.

As Jack lay there, he tried to gather his thoughts. That first judo move he did had worked brilliantly. Ninja number one wasn’t expecting that kind of manoeuvre from a kid.

But it was obvious that this second guy was skilled in judo too. Ninja number two had just pulled a ‘belt drop’ on Jack. There was no way he was going to be able to keep this up forever.

Both men were now standing over him. Jack was going to have to think of a distraction to get out of their clutches.

As the men bent down to pick him up, Jack lifted his Watch Phone and turned its face towards the two men. The GPF had just added one more feature to this device, and Jack was going to use it to buy some more time.

He punched the 'flash' button on his gadget and closed his eyes. Instantly, a blinding white light came out of his Watch Phone, temporarily blinding the two men.

'Oww!' they yelled, as they rubbed their eyes.

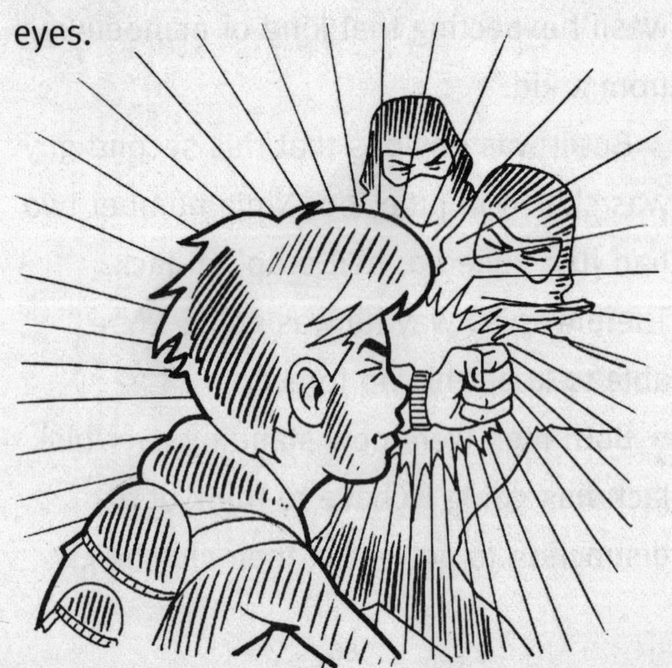

This gave Jack the chance he needed.

He sprinted towards the house, jumped over a shrub and made his way for a drain pipe. Shimmying upwards, Jack climbed it until he reached the edge of the roof. Then, he lifted himself up and over to the tiles.

From this vantage point, he could see everything. By now, Madame Midori had come out of the house and was standing on a patio below Jack.

The ninjas had regained their sight, and were now on the gutter pipe, making their way up to the roof.

Seeing them in these positions gave Jack a brilliant idea. It wasn't often you had a chance like this, thought Jack, to catch three crooks all at the same time. He smiled to himself and reached into his Book Bag. This was going to be fun.

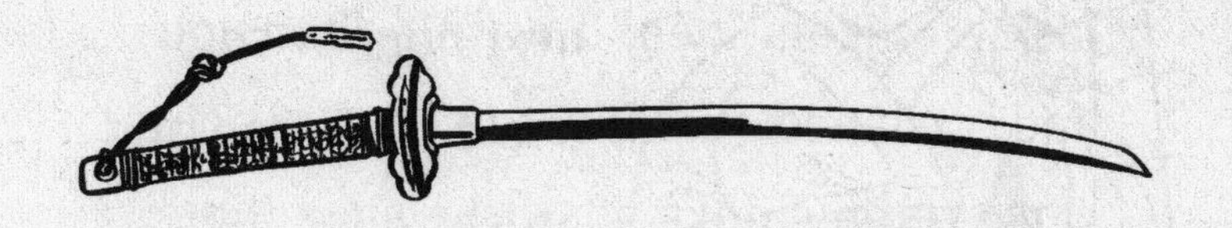

Chapter 17: The Traps

Jack focused on Madame Midori first. He took his Wax Statue dust out of his Book Bag.

He tore open the pack and sprinkled it over her head. As the green dust settled over her hair and body, she became very still. Noises were coming out of her mouth, but she couldn't move her lips.

Since Madame Midori was so fond of herself, Jack figured she wouldn't mind

being turned into a statue, like the kind you'd see in a wax museum. For the next hour or so, she'd be frozen and on show for everybody to see. That is, until the chemical wore off.

Now it was on to those ninjas. Ninja number one had reached the roof. He was running across, kicking tiles off the roof as he went. Jack grabbed one more thing from his Book Bag. This was the called the Gluey Goo.

The Gluey Goo looked like an aerosol can of fake cheese. But inside was some of the stickiest glue you could find. In fact, it could hold the weight of a man, which is exactly what Jack was going to use it for.

He popped the lid, and waited for the ninjas to get close. When they did, he sprayed the glue all over the roof and onto their feet. Within seconds, the Gluey Goo hardened, and the men were stuck in their tracks.

Ninja number one was hopping mad. He tried to step out of his shoes and run away, but the skin on his bare feet got stuck too. He yelped in pain as he tried to get free. But there was no use, he wasn't going anywhere. Jack gave the air a one-two punch in triumph.

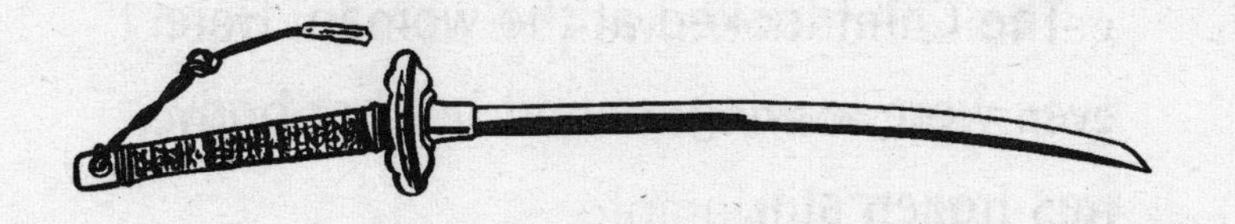

Chapter 18: The Chief Again

In the distance, Jack could hear the sound of sirens. It was the Tokyo police. They were coming to save the day.

When the Chief made his way to the garden, he looked around. There was a frozen woman standing on the back patio, two men sulking under a net and another two glued by their feet to the roof. Needless to say, he was pretty surprised.

'So,' he said to Jack. 'What exactly

happened here?'

'Well,' said Jack. 'Madame Midori masterminded the theft of the treasures and hired these four ninja goons to do it.'

The Chief looked at the woman. Here eyes were moving around but her body was frozen still.

'Hmmm,' he said to Jack. 'Any chance of turning her back to normal? It'll be a bit difficult getting her to sit down in the back of the police car like that.'

'Yeah,' said Jack. He couldn't help but giggle. 'She'll be all right. The effects of the dust only lasts an hour.'

'What about those guys?' asked the Chief. He was pointing to the ninjas stuck to the roof.

'Just spray some water on the glue and it will release the men,' said Jack.

Chief Ito ordered his men to get the hose. As they sprayed ninja number one and the other guy, the men slipped off of the roof and fell onto the ground. After wrestling with the police officers, they were eventually scooped up and carried away.

He could hear ninja number one shouting at him in the distance.

'I'm going to get you ...,' he said, his voice trailing off.

'And these?' said the police chief, nodding in the direction of the men being held by Jack's Net Tosser.

'No problem,' said Jack. He tapped a few commands into his Watch Phone. The net retracted itself and the men were set free. Well, not exactly. Police officers swarmed over them, put some cuffs on and then carried them away too.

'Well,' said Chief Ito. 'It looks like you've solved the crime. The country of Japan can't thank you enough.'

'No worries,' said Jack humbly. 'It's my job. The treasures are in the house. They're stashed away into cardboard boxes.'

Chief Ito thanked Jack again, and the two of them said their farewells. Jack walked across the garden and towards the house. As he passed Madame Midori he looked up at her. Her eyes were

moving frantically back and forth. She was trying to say something to Jack.

'I know,' said Jack. 'You're trying to tell me 'thank you'. It's my pleasure to have captured you and help send you to jail.'

Jack gave her a wink and then walked off. He could hear Madame Midori screaming inside. That wasn't what she wanted to tell Jack. Jack had done his job and he was proud of himself. Yet another collection of criminals behind bars.

He smiled as he walked down the road and found a peaceful public garden, away from Madame Midori's house and the goings on of the police department.

He reached into his Book Bag for his Portable Map. Whenever a secret agent was away on a mission there were many choices for getting home. You could find a real map and put a small flag on it. You could use an 'H' button over the ground button on a lift. If you were underwater in The Egg, you could program 'home' as your destination. Or, you could use this – a small wooden foldout map that looked like your Magic Map at home.

Jack opened it on the ground and waited for the light inside England to glow. As it grew brighter, Jack yelled 'Off to England'. Within moments, Jack was transported home.

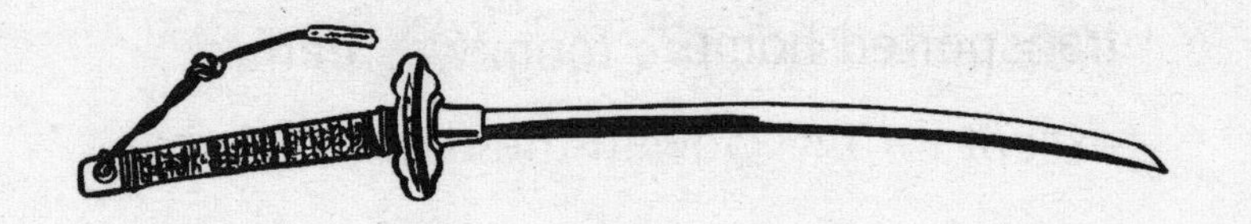

Chapter 19: The Starry Wish

When he arrived, Jack's bedroom was just as he left it. Whizzy was snoozing on Jack's bedside table and his Magic Map was still on the wall. On his desk was a copy of The Samurai, the book he'd been reading about before his latest adventure.

He packed it away in his school backpack, since he'd have to return it to the school library tomorrow. Knowing it was time to get ready for bed, Jack brushed his teeth, yelled goodnight to his parents downstairs and got himself dressed.

Crawling into bed, Jack turned out his side table light. The room was dark, except for the glow-in-the-dark stars that were stuck to the ceiling above him. Jack remembered his Dad giving both he and Max a set of these stars when Jack was six and Max was eight. They took turns with their Dad sticking them in just the right place.

As Jack lay there remembering these happy times, he couldn't help but think about his brother. With Max gone, there was no one to talk to about his missions. And no one to yell 'goodnight' to besides his Mum and Dad.

Closing his eyes, Jack wished on the stars above. He asked whoever was listening to give him another clue about his brother. With any luck, that critical piece of information was just around the corner. Who knows, thought Jack, as he drifted off to sleep, maybe that clue will come tomorrow.